**THIS HALLOWEEN BOOK
BELONGS TO**

....

....

HEY DUGGEE

LADYBIRD BOOKS

UK | USA | Canada | Ireland | Australia | India | New Zealand | South Africa

Ladybird Books is part of the Penguin Random House group of companies
whose addresses can be found at global.penguinrandomhouse.com.

www.penguin.co.uk   www.puffin.co.uk   www.ladybird.co.uk

 Penguin
Random House
UK

First published 2023
001

Text and illustrations copyright © Studio AKA Limited, 2023
Written by Lauren Holowaty

Printed in China

The authorized representative in the EEA is Penguin Random House Ireland,
Morrison Chambers, 32 Nassau Street, Dublin D02 YH68

A CIP catalogue record for this book is available from the British Library

ISBN: 978-1-405-95383-2

All correspondence to:
Ladybird Books, Penguin Random House Children's
One Embassy Gardens, 8 Viaduct Gardens, London SW11 7BW

 MIX
Paper from
responsible sources
FSC
www.fsc.org   FSC® C018179

DUGGEE

THE HALLOWEEN BADGE

ROLY NORRIE HAPPY TAG BETTY

It's Halloween, and Duggee and the Squirrels are decorating the clubhouse.
"Woof woof!" says Duggee. Splendid job, Squirrels!
Everything is looking very spooky.

"Duggee," says Betty, "do we have any treats for our trick-or-treating friends? They'll be here soon!" Oh dear. Duggee has been so busy decorating that he forgot all about trick-or-treating!
But fear not, Squirrels . . .

Duggee has his **Halloween Badge!** He knows how
to make delicious Halloween treats.
"Yay!" cheer the Squirrels. "Can *we* help, Duggee?"
"Ah-woof!" says Duggee. That would be most
SPOOKTACULAR!

Before the Squirrels can start baking, there's something very important they have to do first.

Now Duggee and the Squirrels are ready to start baking.
"What are we going to make?" asks Tag.

"Yes, but what kind?" asks Norrie.
"Won't everyone like *different*
treats?" says Betty.

"Ah-woof!" says Duggee. Great thinking,
Betty. They can make lots of special treats –
something different for everyone!

Duggee and the Squirrels think carefully about their friends and what they like to eat. Then, they race around the kitchen collecting ingredients.

CRASH!

BANG!

Great work, Squirrels! It's time to get baking.

"All finished!" announces Norrie.
But oh dear. Duggee is covered in flour.

AH-WOOOOOOO!

"Nice costume, Duggee!" says Roly.

Just then, they hear . . .

DING-DONG!

"There's somebody at the door!" cheer the Squirrels.

Hooray! The first trick-or-treaters have arrived.
It's Mr and Mr Crab!

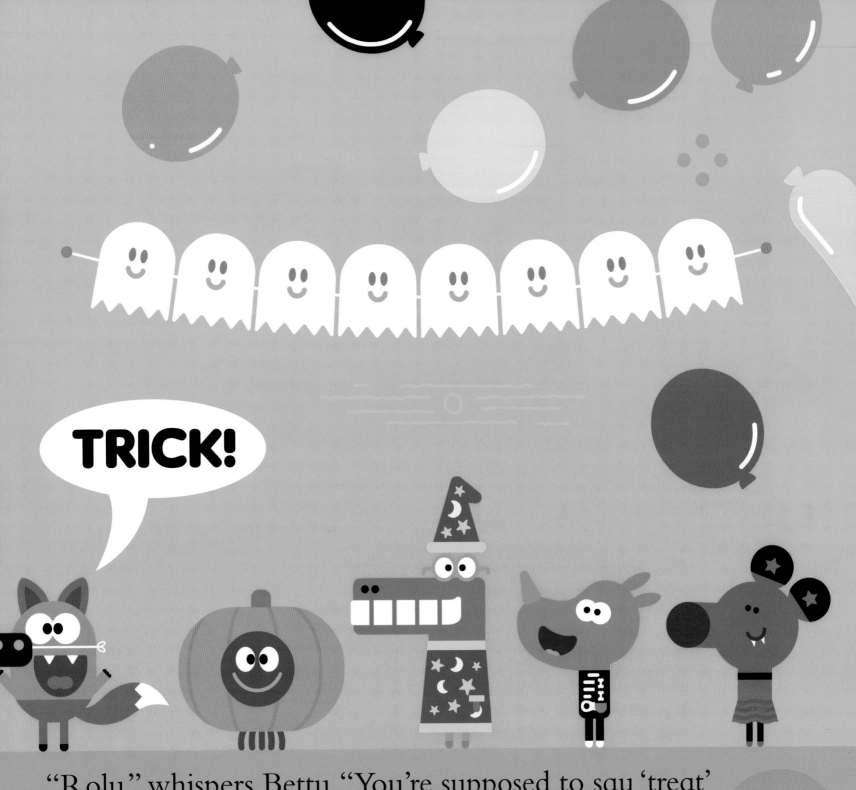

"Roly," whispers Betty. "You're supposed to say 'treat' so we can give them the special treats we made."
"Oh yeah," says Roly. "TREAT!"

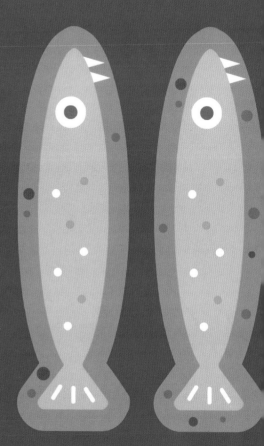

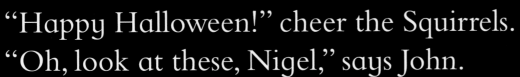"Happy Halloween!" cheer the Squirrels.
"Oh, look at these, Nigel," says John.
"Aren't they fabulously spooky?"
Nom! Nom! Nigel agrees.

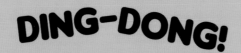
DING-DONG!

"There's somebody at the door!"
cheer the Squirrels.
It's . . .

"THE CHICKENS!" shouts Roly. "Here are your
spoooooooky seedy treats, chickens."

DING-DONG!

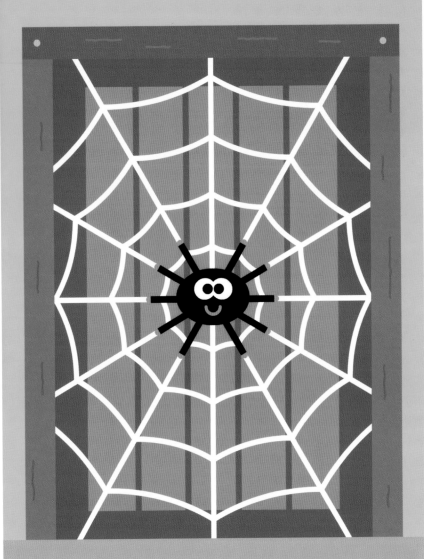

"There's somebody at the door!" the Squirrels cheer again.
It's . . .

"Naughty Monkey!" says Happy. "Here are your banana ghost treats, Naughty Monkey."

DING-DONG! DING-DONG!

It's Chew Chew at the door . . . with a ghost sheep,
Hedgley the hedgehog, Frog AND the rabbits!

"Pumpkin biscuits for you, Chew Chew!" says Tag.

"Glow-in-the-dark grass for you, sheep!" says Betty.

"Creepy-crawly chocolates for you, Hedgley and Frog!" says Roly.

"And frightening carroty finger treats for you, rabbits!" says Norrie.

DING-DONG!

DING-DONG!

DING-DONG!

Soon, EVERYONE is trick-or-treating at the clubhouse!

"We've heard this is the best place in town for treats,"
says a puffing polar bear. He has come all the way
from the North Pole!

"*Beep! Beep! Bop!*" say the aliens. They want to try
the Squirrels' out-of-this-world treats too.

What's that noise now, Squirrels? *Ahhh* . . . the sound of silence.
No more trick-or-treaters!

Well, that was a busy Halloween, Squirrels.
Wouldn't you agree, Duggee? Duggee . . . ?
"Where's Duggee?" asks Tag.

"Duggee!" cheer the Squirrels.
Norrie sees that Duggee has something behind his back.

Happy Halloween! Duggee has made some special treats just for the Squirrels.
"Thanks, Duggee!" they say.
Haven't the Squirrels done well today, Duggee?

They have definitely earned their special treats and their **Halloween Badges!**

Now there's just time for one last thing before the Squirrels go home.

"DUGGEE HUG!"